INTERTWINED

Illustrations by Dorielle Retemyer

First published 2010.

ISBN-13: 978-0692969809

INTERTWINED

A Collection of Short Stories

By

Sherene Noble

Acknowledgements

I owe a debt of gratitude to Enid Joaquin and Ronald J. Daniels. Without your help this project would not have come to fruition. Thank you.

For Lindiwi and Kashka

Table Of Contents

INTERTWINED

Turn Back The Hands of Time

Michelle strolled breezily along Main Avenue, her long black tresses flowing in the crisp afternoon breeze, her face aglow with joy and anticipation.

She was going to meet him!

She had planned carefully for today, taking special care with her hair and her makeup. She took even greater care to ensure that her husband did not know what she was up to.

As her mind dwelled on her husband, she unconsciously caressed her tummy. She was thrilled by the joy of creation that had taken place there, the new life that had budded and was now growing in her womb. He did not know about this either.

Her yellow and white sundress matched her mood and set off her slender, model-like frame well. In a few short months she would be a pumpkin on stilts, not that she would mind. The joy of becoming a mother again far outweighed anything she could possibly look like in the process.

She quickened her step as the café where she was meeting him came into view. Her smile widened when she spotted the dashing, distinguished looking man, dressed casually in a white linen shirt and jeans just like he said he would be.

She walked over to him and touched his arm. His face lit up as he propelled himself out of the lounge chair he had just moments before been casually sprawled across.

She threw herself into his arms, hugging him, squeezing him, kissing him. People stared at them, some with bemused expressions, others clearly irritated by the public display of affection. She didn't care! This was a man she loved, a man whom she had waited for a long time. Now she was ecstatic.

* * *

Michelle drove her car into the garage and stepped out. She was indeed very happy. She couldn't wait to get inside the house so that she could give her husband the news. She could imagine how he would feel. She wished her daughter were home now so that the entire family would be present for her disclosure, but she was too excited to wait until Anecia returned home from school. For now, she would share the good news with only her husband.

She hurried up the front stairs and burst through the door.

"Nicholas!" she called out to her husband as she stepped through the front door. "I'm home! I've got some news for you!"

The blood rushed into Nicholas' head, infusing him with hatred and an urge for violence he had never before imagined possible.

This bitch! This beautiful cold-hearted bitch! Didn't she realize how much she was hurting him?

For some weeks now he had suspected that she was being unfaithful to him. The indicators were numerous - the whispered telephone conversations, the secret smiles which faded when she realized that he were around, the covert excursions to God knows where.

Today he had followed her, a beautiful gay butterfly fluttering in the wind of her new found love. Oh, what a fool he had been! He had seen them embrace. That man had wrapped his arms around his Michelle, his bitch of a wife! Now she was going to pay.

She was still smiling when she laid eyes on his face, a palette of black stormy thoughts lurking just below the surface.

"Nicholas, what's the matter? You look strange, awful!"

Nicholas lunged towards her, lips stretched back in a feral snarl.

"You cheating bitch!" he raged.

The wide curve of her lips changed to a horrified "oh" as she spotted the knife in Nicholas' hand. Shock made her stand shock still and she didn't scream when the serrated edge of the wicked weapon was plunged hilt deep into her chest. Madness seemed to envelop Nicholas as he stabbed and stabbed and stabbed. He was in a frenzy now! He knew she was dead but he could not stop himself.

Somewhere in the distance, an insistent shrilling sound beckoned him. The sound invaded his consciousness, momentarily subduing the voices in his head. Like an automaton, Nicholas picked up the telephone and listened, as a disconnected voice from somewhere deep inside him, a voice he did not know, said hello to the person on the other end.

"Nicholas! You must be Nicholas!" the excited chatter burst through the line. "Has Michelle shared the good news yet? I am so happy today. I have found my long lost daughter and in the process gained a son and a granddaughter and another on the way. Am I not the luckiest man alive?"

A moment's sanity displaced the madness that had taken residence in Nicholas' head.

"Who are you?" he enquired of the caller.

"I'm Michelle's father. Hasn't she told you yet? We met today after years of my trying to track her down. We have been talking on the telephone but finally today, we met. She wanted to surprise you but I guess I called too early. I'm too excited! Now I have Michelle and you and Anecia and the baby. I have found her and she's married and pregnant!" the caller raved.

The telephone slipped from Nicholas' fingers but he failed to notice.

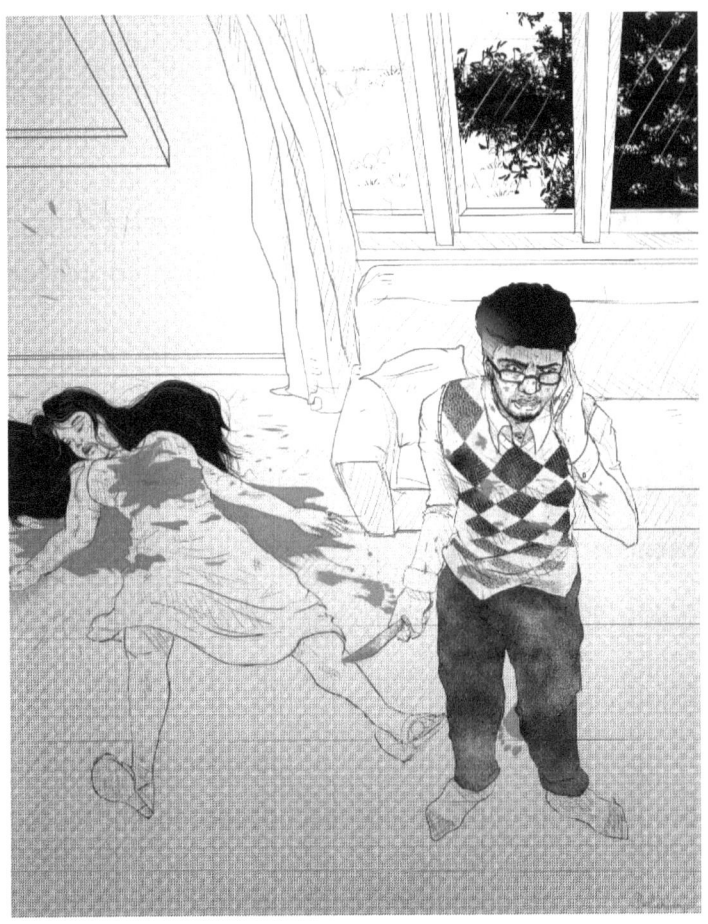

Madness once again became the dominant force in his brain. The noises in his head became deafening. What had he done to his Michelle? The mystery man was her father? Nicholas was beside himself. To think he thought she was being unfaithful! She was pregnant! Is that why she had been sneaking around? Had this whole clandestine operation been a grand scheme to surprise him? Nicholas cradled his head in his hands. To think he thought she was having an affair!

He heard a voice screaming Michelle's name. He yelled at the voice to stop but it wouldn't; it merely screamed back at him, "Look what you've done!"

He ran to her, entreating her to speak to him but the only answer he got was the angry red wounds reproaching him, her eyes piercing the nothingness into which they stared.

As he made his final descent into the pits of madness, he heard the beeping of the bloodied telephone indicating that the caller had hung up.

*   *   *

Snake In The Grass

Lisanne stared anxiously at the strip as she waited for the liquid to saturate it. Two bars meant positive, one…negative. She dreaded a positive result but she was almost sure it would be. She had missed her period and while that in itself was not cause for alarm, she was experiencing what she felt sure was morning sickness. Her mother had already noticed but she had staved off any invasive questioning by pretending that it was a flu bug.

Her parents, Raymond and Constance Chance, would be devastated if they knew that she was pregnant. She was their pride and joy, their darling little baby girl. Her being pregnant would shatter the carefully cultivated pristine image of her family.

Her parents were late starters in the family extension department. They had put starting a family on the back burner to career and self-development. When they were finally ready to start a family, family wasn't ready for them; and she, Lisanne, was long in coming. Her mother was almost forty three and had already given up on conceiving;

her father was forty five, when the miracle of her birth finally occurred.

Needless to say, she was doted on, fawned upon and hopelessly spoilt. She knew that if she were pregnant, life in their household would never be the same again.

Lisanne looked at the strip again. She heard an agonizing groan bouncing off the tiled walls of her carpeted bathroom. She glanced around quickly, only to realize the sound was coming from her. She tried desperately to control herself but the moans were born in the very pits of her womb and forced their way up, wracking her stomach on their way out.

*   *   *

Lisanne first became conscious of what she looked like when she was about eleven years old.

At ten, she had been a string bean of a child, tall for her age but skinny, gangly. Then she began menstruating and her body began to acquire curves and crevices where previously there existed only lines, angles and edges. She had rounded in all the right places.

She stood before the mirror.

She had been splashing around in their swimming pool one Saturday afternoon when she glanced up to discover John - the family's chauffeur handyman gofer and confidant - leering at her. She involuntarily wrapped her arms around herself and shuddered in disgust as he tried unsuccessfully to hide the bulge in his pants. Without a word, she grabbed her towel and hastened to cover herself up. In one fluid movement, she exited the pool and hurried into the house and to her bedroom.

She felt as though he had violated her. She rubbed herself so hard that her skin became pink and sore.

Then she stood before the mirror, assessing what had caused John's reaction. It wasn't hard to figure. She was voluptuous; a child in a woman's body. She hadn't even realized that she had grown into the body of a woman. In her innocent mind, she was still a child, running around in her shorts and camis, unmindful of the erotic impact she was having on the minds of those of the opposite sex.

She flung open her closet door and began hastily extracting her shorts, miniskirts, and anything she deemed too revealing. She gathered the pile of clothes and began stuffing them into garbage bags. She would have her mother take them tomorrow to the Salvation Army. Baggy jeans and t-shirts would suffice for now.

She contemplated telling her parents about the incident but John had been their chauffeur for so long that she felt uncomfortable bringing it up. John had always been kind to her and nothing short of a gentleman. The family trusted him completely. What if this were all in her head? How long had he really been watching her? Did she see a bulge indeed or was that her imagination? Maybe she misunderstood.

She decided not to tell. She would wait a bit. If it happened again, she would definitely tell.

*   *   *

It happened shortly after her twelfth birthday. She was left alone with him, which wasn't unusual. He wished her goodnight and kissed her on the lips as usual. Then the kiss became intense. His tongue unexpectedly pushed past her lips and commenced searching the inner sanctums of her mouth.

Lisanne was shocked!   She was aware of this. She was a bright, informed and mature child. They talked about this in school, in Girl's Club and at church. Now it was happening to her! She struggled and tried to cry out but the arms tightened round her and his mouth covered hers, cutting off any sound she might make. She could smell the alcohol on his breath and taste it as well.

With a swift, deft motion, he forced his way into her. Her agonized cry partly escaped their lips. It was a cry of physical and emotional anguish.

Like an animal, he thrashed around inside her, oblivious to the agony he caused, conscious only of the need to satisfy his own pleasure. When at last he spewed his seed, his head seemed to clear a bit and he was horrified at what he had done.

"What have I done? What have I done? You can't let anyone know. Please, please, promise you won't tell. I don't know what got into me. This will never happen again! Please, don't tell. You know what this could do!"

Lisanne didn't tell. She couldn't. She felt dirty, soiled, but worse, she felt guilty. She didn't want anyone to know. It was her fault! She had become aware of the contours of her body and what it did to those of the opposite sex. She heard the comments, some explicit, that boys and men made about her. Worse yet, she knew how her body felt sometimes. She had experimented, running her fingers along the extended labia and savoring the sensations of pleasure that coursed through her. She would never tell!

Life in the Chance's household continued with only a few minor deviations. He stayed away as much as possible. His eyes always avoided hers. On the outside she was Lisanne. Inside a storm raged as anger, guilt, shame and hurt jostled for position in her mind. She prayed each day for passing time to heal wounds. Six months went by and the storm began to subside. Maybe she had a chance of being whole again.

Then it happened again.

This time she fought and kicked and screamed but that only served to unleash an animal brutality towards her. When she quieted down and relaxed, he became gentle and it almost became pleasurable. She quickly learned to take it placidly.

After that night, the visits became regular.

At school Lisanne appeared to be a well-adjusted, normal teenager. She maintained high grades and participated in extracurricular activities, but on the inside she was tormented. A range of conflicting emotions, guilt, anger, hatred and even love, threatened to tear her apart. Yes, even love, because she loved him as was her duty as much as she loved him for the pleasure he brought her. She also hated him for what he had done to her.

That hate fueled a desire for revenge, so Lisanne plotted. She would have her revenge. She would give away her body since he prized it so dearly.

By the end of her second year at high school, she had slept with several different men, and the only thing she cared about was that she didn't know them, or they her.

On Saturdays she left home for the library but as soon as she was dropped off, she doubled round and hit the streets, offering sexual favors to an abundance of willing and eager participants. This way she could hurt him. This way she could exact revenge.

By the age of fourteen Lisanne had lost track of the number of sexual partners she'd had, but she derived a perverse pleasure in adding to it.

*   *   *

Constance paced the floor of the small private hospital she had brought her daughter to. She had sent John to fetch her husband. Hopefully Raymond would soon be there. She needed his support. She was sick with worry.

Raymond Chance, followed by a worried looking John, barged through the entrance just as Dr. Joseph stepped from the examination room into the waiting room.

"My daughter, where is she? How is she? Doc, what is wrong with my child?" Raymond ranted.

"Calm down. She is alive and will live. Come into my office."

Constance took Raymond's arm as they walked into the doctor's office. She couldn't tell if the trembling was coming from him or from her.

"We have conducted a series of tests on Lisanne, Mr. and Mrs. Chance. I don't know how to put this gently, but your daughter is four months pregnant."

The wail that erupted from Constance was nothing to the anguished cry that threatened to rip Raymond's throat apart.

"Nooooo!" Constance screamed in pain. "Oh no!" This can't be! She is just a child. Someone will pay for this!"

"That's the good news Mrs. Chance." Dr. Joseph explained, in as gentle a tone as he could muster.

"Your daughter has been diagnosed positive with HIV."

A defeated looking Constance slumped into the plush seating Dr. Joseph's office provided.

Raymond Chance passed out.

*   *   *

It was all of two weeks later when the family finally caught up with each other as a unit. Avoiding each other and the issues facing them had been their modus operandi. It was their coping mechanism. However, when the chance coming together occurred, the emotions were running too high to avoid a volatile confrontation.

"Who did this to you? Was it John? Was I wrong to trust that bastard? Tell me! Who did you sleep with?"

"John? Never! John was always a perfect gentleman. What do you care anyway?"

"You little wretch!" screamed Constance. "I trusted you! Now look what you've done. After everything your father and I have done for you, everything we've given to you, you embarrass us like this?"

In a fit of rage Constance rushed over to Lisanne and started scratching at her face. An aged Raymond managed to restrain her but he knew the trouble had just started.

Lisanne's eyes blazed as she pulled herself straight, facing her parents down.

"How could I do this to you? How could you do this to me? You were supposed to protect me! Instead you left me at the mercy of this brute that you call your husband and my father! He took my innocence and you were too blind to see, too self-absorbed to be a wife to him or to notice that he was making me his wife!"

A red sea of shame washed over Raymond. As he slumped into the nearest chair, he seemed to shrink before them, becoming a caricature of himself.

An astonished Constance looked from her husband to her daughter in total disbelief. Walking as though burdened by her own weight, she left the room.

When she returned ten minutes later, they were still in the same position she had left them in.

"Is this true Raymond?" she squeaked.

Words did not emit from him but his expression spoke volumes. Constance had her answer.

"No one must know of this. I will find a way to deal with this. This has to be our little secret." Constance urged in a voice steely with resolve, even as she tried to shake a feeling of déjà vu.

Both Lisanne and Raymond nodded in silent agreement. Constance gave Raymond a stare of hatred and disgust, squared her shoulders and left the room.

*   *   *

At The End Of A Rainbow…

Dorette felt naked. She felt that all eyes were upon her and that everyone knew who she was. She had done her best to disguise herself, arranging the long auburn wig in ringlets atop her head and painting globs of makeup as thickly as she could on her face. She almost didn't recognize herself but she was worried that other people might.

It had come to this!

She had tried every avenue but nothing worked. The bills piled up and she simply couldn't make ends meet.

It was not that she was lazy. On the contrary, she worked hard. During the week she worked at the cafeteria at the Ministry and at weekends she took in washing. She budgeted strictly and did a good job of making each dollar stretch. But then that fool Nicholas, whom she had had the misfortune of bearing children for, had been committed to a mental asylum. There ended his support.

It wasn't enough that he had left her with three children to marry that bitch Michelle. No, he had to add to her burdens. He had caught Michelle being unfaithful to him and in a fit of rage he had killed her. Now Dorette was left alone to struggle with the upkeep of her children.

She would never have been unfaithful to him, she knew that. Her loyalty had been unquestioned; but while she was fairly attractive, she was no match physically or intellectually for Michelle so Nicolas dumped her.

Dorette had been sure that his mother would pitch in and help her for she could more than afford it, but that woman had never liked Dorette or her children. Always felt that they were beneath her and her son, and treated them as such. Dorette couldn't believe that someone could be so heartless.

Now, she was killing herself to make ends meet and she was reduced to this. Secret rendezvous with strange men doing unspeakable things for money. When her friend Sharon had first suggested this she was astounded.

"Are you mad?" she had asked, but Sharon had been quite practical about it.

"It's like this Dorette. We sleep with men for love and we get nothing but pain and heartache. At least this way, we could sleep with them for something more tangible."

It certainly did help with the mental aspect of the job. Sharon also taught her a few tricks aimed at shortening the physical encounter. Now she was ready for her first tryst.

Thank God he was quite attractive and seemed sophisticated too.

He was about sixty, almost twice her age, and six feet tall at least. He had well-proportioned limbs and perfectly manicured hands. Moneyed, clearly!

She was a little surprised that this sort of man was involved in this kind of activity but as Sharon had told her, they were usually the worst kinds: stuck at home in relationships with wives too sophisticated to perform even the most basic sexual acts. Women too concerned with being ladies to be women.

He wanted two hours he said, and Dorette braced herself for what might be an arduous first night, but she comforted herself with the thought that at least he was a pleasure to look at.

But Dorette got the shock of her life. He wanted to talk, not have sex. He wanted someone to bare his soul to. Before she knew it they were chatting away like old friends, revealing their innermost secrets and mutual pains. When she told him her story, he took her in his arms and she buried her face in his chest.

"Look at me," he commanded, lifting her chin so she could look into his eyes.

"Some divine being has sent me to you. Don't do this anymore. I will help you. I can afford it. Just be my friend and confidante."

Dorette could not believe her ears. After all her hardships, she could not believe life could suddenly become so easy.

"Godwin is my name. Give me your number. I will call you tomorrow. Go home. I will ensure that you never have to do this again!"

He put her in a taxi and sent her home. Her purse bulged with the money he had given her. She really could not believe she had received so much for nothing from a virtual stranger.

By the next day, she was worried that it hadn't really happened, but the thousands of dollars on her dresser confirmed that it had. Then she convinced herself that he wouldn't call, but he did, overwhelming her to the point of tears. By the end of their conversation that night, Dorette was in love.

*   *   *

Life became a daze for Dorette. Godwin became her tower of strength and financial pillar. Yet he never asked for sex. In fact, he treated her like a doting father to a favorite daughter. He told her she had replaced the daughter he lost.

It was three months after they met that a distraught Godwin visited her home. He had had an exceptionally hard day at the office and had gone home to a greater than usual barrage of naggings, torment and abuse from his wife. He needed to unburden.

After all he had done for her, Dorette was more than willing to oblige, but tonight she was going to do some prodding. She needed sex and she wanted it with him. If she played her cards right, she would wrest him right out of the hands of his bothersome wife. After all, even though she hadn't had to use them, she hadn't forgotten the tricks Sharon taught her.

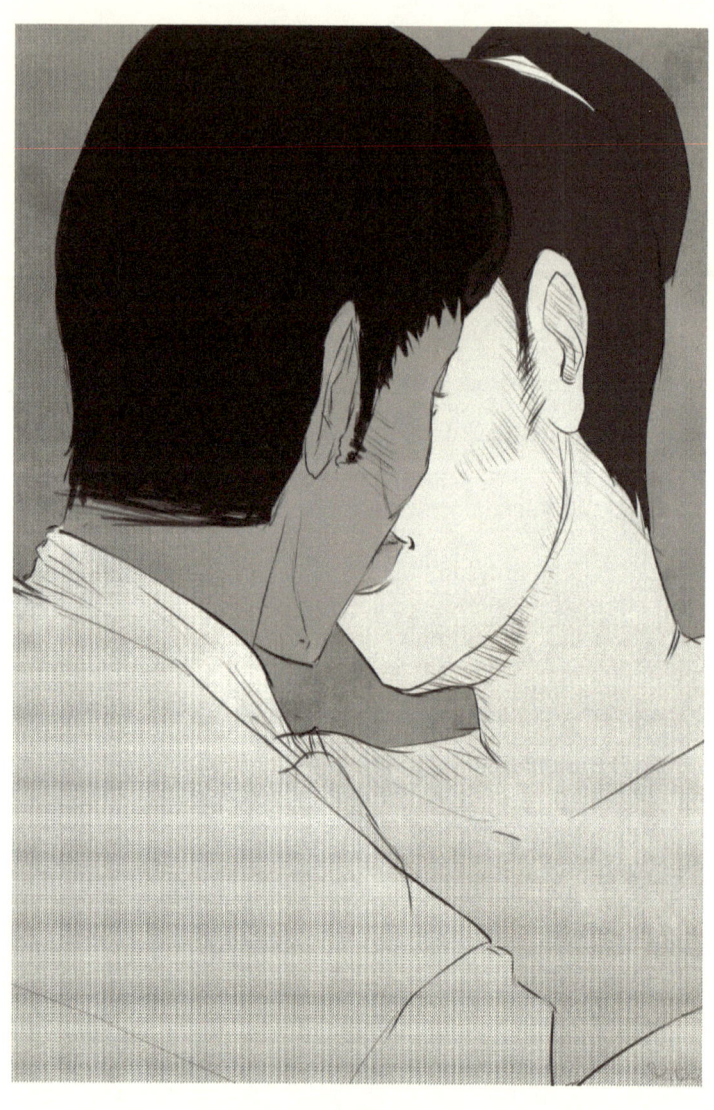

"… drinking from the fullness of her lips"

Before Godwin could realize what was happening, he was in Dorette's arm, drinking from the fullness of her lips. He moved his lips down to savor the delight of her breasts, still firm and supple, despite her three children. They locked in each other's embrace, savoring the sweetness thereof. He was gentle and giving; rough and demanding; forceful and punishing- the unfulfilled seeking fulfilment. She was sore and sweet, and bruised and receiving. The intensity increased to an incomparable ferocity as they rode in a frenzy of uncontrolled passion.

Dorette awoke with a smile on her face and she reached for Godwin but he was gone. He must have awakened during the night and left quietly so as to not disturb her.

She reached down and touched herself. She was still wet and throbbing. Godwin was an amazing lover. She touched herself and let out a startled 'oh' as it occurred to her that she was still so wet because he had ejaculated in her.

"Risky, risky Dorette," she chided herself without conviction. She didn't have a thing to worry about. He was a gentleman. He had his wife and he didn't sleep around.

*   *   *

Dorette sat with her face propped in her hands. What had she done to deserve this? Godwin was on her mind.

The day after they made love, she waited expectantly for his call. It never came. When several days had passed without a word from him, she started to make enquiries but no one knew who she was speaking of.

That was when she realized that she knew absolutely nothing about Godwin. She had been so enamored by him that so many things had slipped by her.

He had played his game to perfection, trapping her into believing him to be virtuous while all along he was nothing but a player with a cruel game.

She had foolishly and carelessly had unprotected sex with him and a pregnancy test had yielded a positive result.

Now, as she sat awaiting the result of an HIV test, she could not shake the feeling that it was a foregone conclusion.

"Dorette Hayles?" the nurse called out her name, "this way please."

It was normal procedure. Positive or negative they counselled you. Somehow she wasn't surprised and remained stoic when the nurse informed her, "I'm sorry, you tested positive for HIV."

*   *   *

Wolf In Sheep's Clothing

It was almost 11:30 pm and the pulsating rhythms of Georgetown could be sensed rather than heard from where Raymond Chance lived.

He completed his toilet, put on his shoes, picked up the keys to the rented SUV which he was using for this occasion, then headed through the door. He walked a short distance to where it was parked a few blocks away, climbed in and assumed another one of his personas. On this occasion he was Godwin Miller - a man with a mission.

On weekends, some parts of the city stayed awake, throbbing with a life of its own. There were party goers, in a kaleidoscope of fashions and vendors selling from coconut water to cocaine. Then there were the vendors of another dispensation peddling their wares. Like butchers offering flesh for sale, they too offered flesh which Raymond wanted to buy. He did not particularly have any real interest in tasting this type of flesh but he had bodily fluids to dispense.

Ever since his daughter's HIV diagnosis and subsequent suicide, he had vowed revenge.

Looking at him, no one would imagine that he was HIV positive, and certainly, no one would deign to imagine that he had contracted it from his own daughter. He seemed a man of character, well above reproach: yet he never even felt guilt at seducing his own daughter. He felt only intense anger that she had shared her delights with someone else; someone who had infected her with a deadly virus.

Someone had infected her. She in turn had infected him. Since he didn't know who that someone was, then, as the saying goes, 'Peter would pay for Paul, and Paul would pay for all'.

When he first started his mission, he had used no guile. His direct approach failed to attract a willing participant. In this day of increased awareness, few prostitutes were willing to provide unprotected sexual favors. Heck, they insisted you wear a condom even for oral sex! Raymond Chance had to get them to let their guard down somehow.

So he developed a strategy. It worked each and every time, with hustlers of both genders. Tonight would be no different.

He drove slowly across King Street and turned left onto the curved portion of road that formed the roundabout that surrounded the cathedral. Scores of young men, some dressed as women, littered the steps of the building. He spotted one he wanted.

His mark on this occasion was a tall, young man of good build. Something about him looked familiar and it was not because he had seen him around on the last three occasions that he had passed the area. Perhaps it was this seeming familiarity that caused him to decide upon him.

Raymond had seen him thrice before but hadn't made a move. Tonight he would close in for the kill.

Mark watched from beneath slit lids as the dapper gentleman in the SUV approached him. His time had finally come. He had waited for this moment for a long time.

"You're on beat tonight?" Mr. Dapper asked him.

"You need a job?" Mark returned.

Dapper smiled. You didn't ask potential hook-ups such questions. In this business you couldn't be too careful.

"I need to talk. I need a friend."

""You need a job?" Mark returned."

Mark climbed into the sleek SUV.

"I'm Godwin," said Mr. Dapper.

Mark smiled again. The name seemed to match the persona. He did seem like some kind of God.

"I'm Rawle." Mark returned.

They both looked at each other and grinned knowingly. It was understood. In this business real names were rarely disclosed.

"Where are we going Godwin?"

Godwin stared at Rawle for a long time. Rawle was a beauty! Rawle possessed light, very clear skin. His eyes were large, round and midnight black. His eyelashes were straight and amazingly long. He had a way of fluttering them unto his cheek in a very effeminate manner.

"Whatever is your preference Rawle?" I want to please you."

"Let's go to the sea wall. Some cool air in the early part of the night always makes for a better latter half."

"The seawall is packed with 'patrons' on the weekend. We wouldn't be private." Godwin declined.

"I know a spot where we can be private. The sound of the sea will set the tone for later."

"I just want to talk Rawle." Godwin reaffirmed.

Rawle looked at him for a long moment.

"Sure if you insist."

Raymond wondered what Rawle would do if he knew he had just been fed a baited line.

*   *   *

Rawle was right! The spot was secluded! There wasn't another vehicle there, nor it seemed, was there another person. It was as though, in a few minutes' drive they had been completely removed from human existence. It was an ideal spot for this sort of secret rendezvous. Yet, somehow Raymond felt uncomfortable.

"Must we stay here?" he asked, trying to hide his apprehension from his companion.

"Not if you don't want to. Don't you like it here?"

"It's just so isolated."

"But isn't that just what you need? There's nothing to worry about. It's just me and you here. But we can go if you want to," Rawle reassured.

Raymond was beginning to feel a little silly.

"Never mind," he said uncertainly, "we'll stay."

Somehow he failed to shake off that nagging feeling.

Raymond was somewhere in the middle of the tale he spun for these occasions when he began to sense that something was horribly wrong. The hairs on the back of his neck stood on end and his spine tingled. He stopped mid-sentence and turned to look at Rawle.

The knife in Rawle's hand ripped across his belly and blood spurted out in a stream.

"This is for Dorette! You remember Dorette don't you Mr. Raymond Chance?"

Raymond's eyes bulged.

"I'm Mark Hayles. Dorette's brother. You do know she got a daughter by you, along with your deadly virus?"

The knife flashed again and this time he felt his innards tumble out in his hands.

Mark looked at him with an expression devoid of sympathy. He wondered what strange twist of events could have converted this apparent model of a man into a maniac; a madman with a dangerous quest.

Raymond stared sightlessly down at the foul mess in his hands, oblivious to a third flashing of the knife ending in a puncture in the left side of his chest. As his life ebbed, he couldn't help thinking how ironic it was that he had thought he was the one closing in for the kill.

*   *   *

The vagrant had been able to give an excellent description of Raymond's killer but Mark had already shed the false lashes and wig that had been part of his disguise. After a few months, his body had regained its original skin tone. He had executed his plan to perfection. The police had no reason to even look in his direction.

*   *   *

Full Circle

Constance Chance stepped out of her car and strolled purposefully towards the courthouse. She had another big case which was concluding today. After this, she would get some much needed vacation.

Ever since her daughter's death and her husband's murder, she had been working unceasingly, trying to bury her woes in piles of case files, delaying the inevitable; the day she would have to confront the emotions and psychological issues of the recent events in her life.

Eventually, she overloaded.

During a particularly volatile trial, she had snapped, screaming at the judge, the prosecutor, and everyone else in the courtroom.

She was restrained and rushed to one of the country's best private hospitals, where she spent three weeks of medicated bliss. At the end of her sojourn, she felt better mentally and headed straight back to work, but soon she was feeling burnt out physically.

She called her airline and booked a ticket to Saba, a lovely Caribbean island in the Netherland Antilles. She would go there and unwind.

She imagined herself in bikini, dark sunglasses and wide brimmed straw hat, strolling the sandy beaches: swimming in the azure waters of the Caribbean Sea: lolling on beach chairs with novel in hand: sipping margaritas and Pina-coladas: being ogled by island men on the lookout for a rich woman to spread a few dollars around. Beach bums they called them.

Constance, immersed in the visualizations of her relaxing holiday, missed the hole on the pavement into which her shoe heel caught, sending her sprawling into the road.

"There you go, steady now!"

The words came from her knight in shining armor, a young man who had just saved her from sure injury had he not broken her fall. She was slipping figuratively and literally.

"Thank you! I'm sure I would have skinned my poor knees at the very least." She laughed nervously.

Constance straightened her clothes but was still shaken and unsteady.

"Here, take my arm. Let me help you to where you're going. You're unsteady."

Constance was reluctant but when her knees refused to bear the burden of her weight, she was forced to accept his help.

Once settled in her office, she thanked him again.

"Could I get you something for your help sir?"

"Not at all. It was nothing. It's not every day that I get to save a lovely young lady from disaster," he returned lightly.

"Well at least let me buy you lunch, then. If you're not busy call me at noon," she insisted.

"Very well then." The younger man answered as he took the card she proffered. The young man left and Constance was soon engrossed in her work, never giving further thought to the incident, until her phone rang at twelve.

"Hello this is Mark."

"Who is this?" she asked in a coldly professional tone.

"Mark, the guy from this morning." He responded, faltering at the frost in her voice.

"Oh, I'm sorry; I didn't get your name this morning. Where can I pick you up?"

By the end of the lunch date, the young man had so knocked Constance off her feet that she impulsively booked a ticket to Saba for him as well.

This was totally out of character for her. He was way below her social level and he could have been her son! Ordinarily, she wouldn't spare him a second glance.

When she had fallen earlier on, she started thinking that everything seemed to be going wrong for her but from there, things began steadily improving. Her intentions were to have a quick lunch as a polite thank you and then forget about her 'savior'; but in the more relaxed atmosphere of the restaurant, she had a chance to observe him. It was the first time in a long time she had looked at a man in that way. He was attractive! She felt stirrings she long thought dead in places she had forgotten existed for those reasons.   It was clear that the attraction was mutual for though she was an older woman, she kept herself well and dressed quite nicely.

Everything about this was against social conventions but, what the heck?

"So what? After all I've been through, I deserve a break," she convinced herself, smiling at the bawdy unintentional pun. Besides, no one would know them in Saba and she would return to being a highly respected senior partner in the country's most prestigious law firm and he to his job as an electrician. No one would be the wiser.

Tomorrow, she and Mark were headed to Saba.

*   *   *

The landing at the Juancho E. Irausquin airport was exhilarating. It had the shortest runway she had ever seen in all her years of travel. On each side of the runway were steep hills. The hills ended in cliffs that dropped sharply into the sea. It made for an exhilarating entrance into the island.

Saba was all it was mapped out to be and more. From obsequious customs officials at the airport to the fawning staff at the Queen's Garden Resort, Constance knew she was about to be pampered. They had scarcely settled into their suite when they were locked in each other's embrace. She had thought that the intimacy between them would be awkward, his being younger than she was, but it turned out to be the most natural thing in the world.

Their lovemaking was intense, fiery, volcanic, and when she erupted, Mount Helena would have been envious. She felt alive, rejuvenated. She was insatiable, wanting more, and more and more. And Mark was a stallion incarnate. He was up to the task, fulfilling her every desire.

The first few nights were sheer bliss. She just couldn't seem to get enough of him. One night, as they lay sated in each other's arms, a thought occurred to Mark.

"You do realize we've been careless all this time right?" he asked Constance.

She sprang up. It hadn't even occurred to her! She was so caught up in the desires of the flesh that she didn't even remember precaution. What had she done! Her carelessness had just condemned this innocent man to death! It was not intentional, but it had happened.

"Relax though," he comforted her, pulling her back unto the bed. "You don't have a thing to worry about, I'm quite safe. I play it safe and still get tested every three months. And you of course, don't sleep around."

She lay sated in his arms.

Constance shuddered as the full force of the realization hit her like a bolt of lightning. No, she didn't sleep around but her husband had.

"Whoa! Still orgasmic! Now that's good for my ego!" Mark laughed.

"You know you're a great lover and you don't need me to tell you that!" she responded, "and if the chemistry is right between two people, then the lovemaking is even better."

The words were right but the tone was all wrong. She was definitely worried. He sought to reassure her, wrapping his arms tightly around her and drawing her closer to him, if that were even possible.

"Baby it's all good I promise you."

Mark reached for her again, and her traitorous, covetous body responded of its own accord, ignoring the compendium of confused thoughts creating havoc in her mind.

*   *   *

They were having a late breakfast, chatting about this, that and nothing in particular.

"I can't understand this," he was saying to her, "I just feel this deep connection to you. It's as if I've known and loved you for a long, long time. Tell me you feel it too, do you?"

She nodded. As much as she hated to admit it, it was true. She did feel an unusual attachment to him but she wasn't about to let it develop into something she couldn't control. She really needed to get a grip of herself. This was just a quick fix, a fix that had already gone terribly, terribly wrong.

"Tell me about your husband? Was there this type of connection between you two?"

The talk of her husband brought back to her mind the thoughts she had been pushing away for the past few nights. Constance was reluctant to speak for fear that the horror of her actions would be evident in her tone. It had not been deliberate. She had simply been so mired in her own desires that she had failed to do what she needed to do. Now she made this young man an unwitting victim, but she couldn't tell him now.

He sensed her reluctance and was just about to speak again when she responded.

"He was killed, just about two years ago. Three stab wounds, including one to the heart; they never found his killer and we…"

A strangled, haunted cry escaped Mark's lips.

"What's the matter darling?" Constance asked, turning to look at him.

"I... I ... I…." He had to be calm here. He couldn't give himself away. This was one double whammy.

"I… I feel your pain."

"Pain! I don't feel one iota of sympathy for him! He got what he deserved. We always do. I'd like to thank the person who did it." Her voice was harsh, unfeeling.

Mark tucked his hand under his head and stared up at the ceiling.

Life was indeed a bitch!

Two years ago he had killed Raymond Chance for knowingly infecting his sister with HIV. He didn't get caught for killing Raymond, but Raymond sure did get him in the end.

*   *   *

Intertwined

The sun's pale smile faded as dusk enveloped the tired city. At an open window of the Ocean Bay Guest House on the East Coast Public road, an equally tired Gordon Merchant sighed as the final vestiges of sunlight surrendered to the night. His weariness was inherent in his soul, a result of his youthful errors and events of his recent past. That things could have gone so dismally wrong was inconceivable, but they had. How could fate be so twisted? He wondered if she knew.

He was just twenty years old when they met. She was fifteen, with the world at her fingertips. She was the apple of her parent's eyes. Their only child, she was pampered and spoiled.

He was surprised that she had even spoken to him. Her class didn't mingle with his class. He fell in love with her.

She wasn't sure that what she felt was love. Perhaps he presented an opportunity for her to be naughty, to rebel against the very staid, very proper upbringing that had been hers.

She was experiencing the power she read about in books, the power and pleasure white women derived from bedding the 'slaves' for the resultant sense of dominion it gave them.

She had read Harriet Jacob's slave narrative, *Incidents in the Life of a Slave Girl*. Jacobs related the tale of a neighboring slave owner whose daughter selected the meanest of his slaves to father her child. It was this tale that fueled her desire for him.

No, she wasn't white and he wasn't a slave. Slavery was long since abolished but their social rank set them apart.

She loved that this person of lesser standing groveled at her feet and she exercised her superiority, ordering him around, making him do whatever she wanted.

Her parents would never imagine that their darling angel possessed a side to her that would pale Jezebel. Gordon didn't recognize it either; he was in love.

One careless liaison was all it took to reveal the illicit union. By the time she realized she was pregnant it was all too late. Her parents being who they were, were anxious to avoid a scandal. The matter was hushed, the necessary arrangements made and she was sent off to Guyana to complete her gestation.

Once the baby was born, it would be offered for adoption. Then she would return home, innocent and pure to the uninformed mind; and to him, for to him she could only be but an angel.

But to Cary and Beverly Winthrop, she was a symbol of their failure as parents, the only thing they had failed at it seemed.

Several months later, she had written to say that she was staying in Guyana. The Winthrops did everything they could to convince her to return but she knew only how to have her own way. Eventually, they pledged to support her until she could stand on her own feet but to have nothing further to do with her.

Gordon on the other hand was elated. It meant that she intended to keep the baby. He would raise some money, travel to Guyana, and they would make life there. He would be a husband to her and father to his son, for he was sure it was a boy.

But she had proven to be as ambitious and callous as her parents. She had sent him a card containing two pictures, one of a baby boy and the other of a baby girl, along with a note to say that she had given them up for adoption. She couldn't be a mother at sixteen! She wanted only to be left alone to pursue her dreams, which he had temporarily interrupted.

What the hell else did he expect? She was a Winthrop!

He was plunged into a debilitating abyss of pain.

For years he had staggered through life, but eventually, gradually, he pulled himself together, fitting the pieces of his life back together again. Now he was worthy and even thankful for his experiences of the past as those had shaped a strong character. He strolled in high society, rubbed shoulders with substance for he was substantial. But in his heart, there always lingered a yearning to unite with his seed.

Finally he made the decision. He commenced his search, armed with pictures of a baby boy and girl, both now no longer babies, but he a man and she a woman.

"They would be thirty-four now," he mused.

It didn't take long for him to find her. He did!

She was more than he expected but less than he got; for on the very day he finally met her, she died. Died! A euphemism for the senseless murder that rendered poor Michelle's body lifeless! Her husband had stabbed her fifty seven times!

He found then that he was not that tough after all, for her death had brought a pain akin to that her birth had engendered.

He couldn't bring himself to attend her funeral. He kept his distance, wanting to remember her as he last saw her, beautiful and full of life. He wanted to remember her as she was alive.

It seemed his liaisons with them were destined for tragedy. This thought almost dissuaded him from finding his son.

A year passed before he recommenced his search, feeling that he had to go on. He was saddened by the knowledge that his son, if he found him, would never know his twin sister.

*   *   *

Euphoria was too mild a word to describe Gordon's state of mind. He bounded across the little bridge and practically leapt up the stairs of the house that was home to his son.

When he had spoken with his son's adopted mother, she seemed guarded, reluctant to speak on the phone. She insisted on talking in person. That he could understand.

Now as he rang the doorbell, his heart did the samba in his chest and he felt lightheaded with joy and anticipation.

The door swung open and a small woman with hung shoulders stood before him. Wordlessly, she took the picture from his outstretched hands and gazed at it for a long while. Her face twisted in pain and Gordon's heart missed a step in its choreographed rhythms.

"Is it not my son?" he asked, in a voice that sounded like it belonged to a stranger.

"Yes this is my son." She paused for a bit then continued, "Your son."

She turned away, plodding to a nearby chair, depositing her body into it.

"Gordon's heart missed a step in its choreographed ..."

"Come in," she said after a while, as though her discourtesy had only just occurred to her.

Gordon's heart slowed. He stared quizzically at her as he took a seat, almost afraid to speak. A palpable tension had crept up and enveloped the room.

"Nicholas is not here." She spoke so quietly he found himself stretching over to catch her words.

"He is in an asylum." She sighed heavily.

It took a while for her words to register in Gordon's mind.

"He killed his wife you know," she continued tonelessly. "He thought she was being unfaithful. He stabbed her fifty seven times."

A white hot poker seared Gordon's chest, as a still raw memory killed any remaining hope.

"Michelle! She was such a lovely girl. I don't know what took over Nicholas. My son is a murderer and a madman!"

Gordon was too horrified to speak. His daughter and

his son, brother and sister, caught in a web too intertwined; almost surreal.

Her empty eyes didn't even see him leave and long after he had stumbled blindly from her home, she was still staring blankly, mumbling Nicholas' name.

*   *   *

The Unfortunate

Anecia hastened her steps as she made her way back home. Home was a sprawling expanse of a house, located in Atlantic Gardens, one of the middle class communities in her country. Both her mother and father were from well to do backgrounds and had done well themselves, making for a more than comfortable existence. Now that they were both gone, her mother killed by the hands of her step dad, the victim of a jealous rage; her step dad put away for insanity, she lived with her maternal grandparents, still comfortable, but her mind an inferno of conflicts and emotions.

A thousand questions reverberated in her mind. "Why me?" "Why them?" "What went wrong?"

She wished she had answers but at the same time was thankful that she didn't, for she was sure that the answers were too complex for her puerile mind to comprehend.

Her dad died when she was only four years old, the victim of a tragic accident. Years later, her mother remarried to Nicholas Fortune. It had seemed like they had the perfect relationship but something had gone terribly wrong. Her stepfather, in a fit of jealous rage had killed her mother.

She experienced a tortuous period of denial and rebellion. She took her anger on anything and anyone who happened to be close by at the time. She screamed and threw violent tantrums, ranted and raved.

In one fit of rage, she attacked her Math teacher, hitting him with the broken leg of a desk, causing him several injuries. Her grandparents arranged counselling for her and the matter was quietly settled with sizeable compensation for her teacher. Since then, she resolved to curb those impulses to unleash her anger. She began volunteering at St John's orphanage and it helped her to put her life in perspective. She was learning that in spite of the adversities, she was still luckier than many.

She pushed open the gate and walked into the pretty, tiled yard with its display of potted plants and fountains. She rarely failed to find solace here. The vibrant colors and aesthetics always soothed her. They reminded her of her mother, who spent many of her afternoons gently caring for those flowers.

"Where is granny?" she asked Stephen.

Stephen was their groundskeeper, but he was more like family.

"She's out. Had to leave hurriedly. Said she would be back by eight. Granddad won't be home until late." Since her mother's murder her grandparents had moved into the home.

"Okay, well I will be in my room." Anecia informed him.

"I will leave in another five minutes so have a good night. I will see you tomorrow," Stephen told her.

Stephen's eyes followed Anecia to the house. He knew she would go to her room, put the music on, and cry her little heart out for her parents. His heart ached for her. If only he could bring Michelle and Nicholas back. If only he could comfort her. He had watched her grow, ever since he started working with them seven years ago.

She was just seven at the time and she was such an adorable child. They had connected immediately. He soon became much more than a hired servant. He was a treasured member of the household. He really loved their family; Michelle, Nicholas and Anecia. He was broken up over Michelle and Nicholas but what he saw Anecia going through was even more devastating to him. He longed to comfort her, to hold her just like he did when she was younger, but since that tragic incident she had changed. She had grown cold, aloof.

Stephen packed up, headed for the gate then inexplicably turned and headed back into the house. He felt truly uncomfortable leaving her alone in that brooding house. He silently slipped up to her bedroom. The door was slightly ajar and he peered in. Even in the dark, he could tell that she was crying. He could sense more than see her body shaking violently from the sobs.

He paused for a long while, thinking that it would be highly inappropriate for a man to enter the bedroom of a young lady, especially since she was alone in the house and it was dark. He changed his mind. He had better leave.

*   *   *

Out of the corner of her eye, Anecia spotted the outline of a person about to enter her room. She tried to make the person out. It definitely was a man. He was too short to be her grandfather, and it could not be Stephen for he would have left by now. She couldn't remember locking the front door.

Fear made her tremble. She was alone in this house with an intruder. Vivid imaginings of what could happen to her flashed through her mind. After all that had happened in her life, this could not be happening.

If only she could reach the gun in the bed drawer before he got to her. She had brought it into her room during one of her suicidal moments but had been interrupted by her grandmother. She'd barely managed to slip it under her pillow just as her grandmother entered her room.

Since that incident, her desire to end her life had waned, but an opportunity to return the weapon to her grandfather's hiding place had never presented itself. Now she could see it was providence.

She stretched as discreetly and silently as she could, slipped the weapon out and got a steady grip. She offered a silent prayer of thanks that her bedroom was dark.

She lifted the weapon and pointed it toward the door.

"She slipped the weapon out."

He was still in the doorway. Why wasn't he moving? She started to pull the trigger. At that very moment the door pushed wide open and a hand extended to the light switch. She fired just as the light came on.

Only a gurgle escaped Stephen's lips as he crumpled to the floor.

*   *   *

Mr. and Mrs. Williams knew it was an accident. They knew Anecia would never knowingly hurt Stephen. Stephen treated Anecia like she was his own daughter. They in turn treated him like he was family.

The Police had other notions. These wealthy folks were clearly trying to protect their granddaughter. No doubt were of the opinion that wealthy folks believe that prison was only for the poor and that there was nothing money couldn't buy.

With Anecia's recent history of anger and violence, it was difficult to convince them that she had not murdered Stephen in a fit of rage. They were ready to make examples of these rich folks. The Williams' needed the best damn lawyer money could buy. They needed Constance Chance!

A Second Chance

She stared at the face before her, hoping to discern why it seemed so familiar. The face before her was that of her latest client. A troubled, juvenile face, it was contorted with pain and worry.

It was a face which brought unexpected pain, because as she stared at the young lady sitting huddled before her, the young girl's features struck a chord of familiarity somewhere in her consciousness.

She willed her eyes to stop staring at the face, and continued with her questions while her mind swirled with worrying questions.

She could tell that this child was innocent. What was wrong with the police in this country anyway? With proper police work, she and this girl would have never met. Indeed, her grandparents could have chosen any other lawyer, but some elusive thing in her mind told her it was fate that they did. She was meant to meet this young lady.

She wrapped up her session and walked out of the room, secure in the knowledge that this was one case she would win.

Constance got into her car, kicked her shoes off, took a deep breath and allowed her body to sink into the upholstery seating. She willed her body and mind relax as her chauffeur Roger maneuvered his way through congested mid-afternoon traffic to get to her home, a beautiful split level bungalow in the Bel Air Park suburb of Georgetown.

It was an unusual journey because throughout it, her new client's face haunted her. She searched her mind for a possible explanation but only one thought kept recurring. She entered her house and headed straight to her bedroom, to the vault in the wall where she kept them. They were yellow with age but in otherwise good condition considering that it was thirty five years since she had taken them. Even her husband had never seen them.

There was no mistaking it. Her client was the split, if somewhat mature image of the two faces that smiled up at her. She picked up the phone and dialed a number.

"Henry, I have a job for you. Could you come over now?"

Less than half an hour later, Henry Johnston, the private investigator that she frequently used, was sitting in her living room, his face wearing its usual blank expression. His expression didn't change as she told the story. It was the story of her client who bore an uncanny resemblance to two babies she gave birth to and had given up for adoption thirty four years ago.

"Find them for me!" was her directive to Henry.

*   *   *

She tightened the noose around her neck and prepared to kick away the chair beneath her feet. This is what her life had become! It was a life she no longer wanted to live. For all her successes she was still an abject failure.

In the field of law, she was undisputedly the best but in the field of life she was below the level of scum and it all came crashing home the day she read Henry Johnston's report.

When Henry delivered the report he wouldn't meet her eyes. He just handed it over and cleared out. His actions had filled her with apprehension, but she opened and began reading anyway. That is when she became sure she could never look anyone else in the eyes ever again.

Many years ago, while she was still a teenager, she became pregnant for a young man far beneath her station. In order to avoid the associated scandal, she left her home and came here to Guyana, where she gave birth to twins. She gave them up for adoption and moved on with her life, forgetting about those encumbrances as she thought of them. She stopped using her first name and adopted a new identity and life for herself.

Now her web of secrecy had entangled and doomed so many lives. If only she had the courage to live with her mistakes. She could still have achieved so much, for she was driven by ambition, but she would have had the bonus of two beautiful children and their lives and hers would certainly not have veered on the ugly, tragic course it had.

Henry's report told a sad tale. As she read it, she could almost see her life reel by like the plot of a bad movie.

Here she was, a victim of HIV. The two children she had given up for adoption had unknowingly entered an incestuous marriage. Doomed from the start, that marriage had ended in murder. Her son had killed his sister, thinking that she was being unfaithful to him. Her younger daughter had been sexually abused by her husband right beneath her nose. How could she have missed that? Her daughter had infected her husband with the HIV virus, before eventually committing suicide. Then her husband had been murdered. She had infected and innocent man. Now her newly found granddaughter was charged with murder. God knows what else had happened she didn't know about.

Was there no end to this sick, twisted tale?

The more she thought of it the more she knew what she needed to do. There was an end to it!

Since her life ran like a soap opera, she would end it soap opera style.

Several filled envelopes containing her will, a letter to her newfound granddaughter and one to her parents, lay on her dresser in the corner of her room.

She hoped they would all forgive her.

She kicked the stool from beneath her feet and the noose, like an iron fist, tightened its stranglehold around her neck.

*   *   *

"The noose, like an iron fist, tightened its stranglehold …"

The pristine whiteness of the walls was in stark contrast to the blackness that enfolded Constance in what seemed like moments ago.

Is this what heaven looked like? Shouldn't she be in a place of red walls and blazing heat? Was God this forgiving?

"You're awake!" an elated voice exclaimed, too close to her ear. The face that stared down at her looked vaguely familiar.

"Hello Melody Winthrop, alias Constance Chance."

"Who are you? Where am I? How did I get here?"

"I am Gordon Merchant."

Constance's eyes widened as the name found a place in her memory. This was a name from very far back, from a place in her that she didn't want to revisit.

"I've been trying to find you for quite some time now. You're in the hospital. John and I brought you here three days ago. You tried to kill yourself. We found you in the nick of time.

"And why did you stop me? I don't want to live!" she grated out, her tone a sharp slap.

"Oh yes Melody, go ahead. Take the easy way out as usual. Don't you think it is time you started accepting responsibility for your actions. You're more concerned with image than with life; with how you are perceived than with who you are. Who are you anyway?" Gordon was relentless.

Constance stared hard at the man who fathered her first two children. She was silent for a long time.

He was right!

She had missed out on so much of her life being someone else. Thank God she still had a little life left. Thank God Gordon had found her. Many years ago he had entrusted her with two lives, lives that she had destroyed. Now he had given her back her own.

*   *   *

Ruthel Haynes looked at the elegantly dressed woman with her hands extended, standing before her. She recognized her immediately. She was Constance Chance, Attorney-at-Law extraordinaire.

"Melody Winthrop," the woman said, shaking Sonia's hand firmly. Ruthel looked at her quizzically.

"I'd like to be an advocate for HIV/AIDS awareness. I have a story which you would find pretty interesting. I want to share my story with the public. I hope I can change behaviors and attitudes."

"Thank you Ms. Winthrop. We can use all the help we can get." Ruthel smiled, though still somewhat confused. "Tell me your story."

Melody Winthrop also known as Constance Chance handed her Henry Johnston's report. She didn't have to share all those details with Ruthel, but she wanted to. It was an act of catharsis.

As Ruthel opened the envelop Constance walked over to the open window in Sonia's office at the Aids Program Secretariat and took a deep breath.

Outside, the air was crisp with the freshness of a day still young and the sun beamed gaily down, spreading her glory on the earth's face. Constance felt like the day she beheld.

*   *   *

Never Too Late

Walking late evening in downtown Georgetown was a like strolling through a dumpsite. Garbage from the day's activities littered the streets and the pungent odors of rotting food assaulted the nostrils.

Rats the size of mongooses confidently roamed the streets, with an arrogance that seemed to demand that humans leave the streets to them. Mark Hayles couldn't feel more at home.

He felt like a piece of litter - of the same or lesser value. He had denigrated from one most likely to succeed in life, to one who didn't have much of a life.

At school he was far from being the brightest but he was certainly the most determined.

He worked hard, did everything in his power to improve himself, enrolled at a technical college and, upon leaving, established a thriving business as an electrical contractor. He was good looking and looked good.

Women always found him attractive. Constance Chance, a woman highly esteemed and of unquestionable virtue was one of those. Unfortunately, she was the carrier of a deadly virus.

Who would have believed it? A highly esteemed lawyer, a brilliant mind, a great career, carrying what might be the world's most stigmatized disease!

Mark looked at the young woman walking next to him and sneered. They were all so daft, and so cheap, every one of them. Offer them a few dollars and they would do anything one asked. They couldn't wait for life. They wanted it now; the fancy clothes, parties, hanging with the 'in crowd' while not having the money to do any of those.

He walked her up the stairs of the sleazy hotel, booked a room, and guided her to it.

She couldn't be more than fifteen years old. To think that in a few short years, her life would be over; she'd be another victim of a raging incurable disease that nations all over the world spent billions a year educating people about; while people all over the world, invested time, and sometimes money, doing exactly what they had been warned against. How many times had he not heard the refrains,

'Protect your pleasure', 'Use a condom every time' or 'Get tested'?

He did get tested on numerous occasions and protected his pleasure too, but one unguarded moment with the most unlikely of candidates: one error of judgement and his life was cast in limbo, leaving him at the mercy of a disease that even took away one's dignity.

He looked at the face before him, staring at him in obtuse anticipation. It was a cow's face - timid, bland, revealing the thickness that lay beneath it. Bile rose in his throat and he swallowed hard, trying to resist a sudden, intense, unreasonable impulse to beat the life out of her.

It wasn't her fault that he lost his way. Unfortunately, she was a woman and she represented the woman who had made him sick, and the many women he in turn gave it to. They would carry it on to their partners and continue a vicious cycle of transmission, for a few dollars more or a few minutes of pleasure.

In her he could see Dorette, his sister, who had become a victim of a cunning plot. He remembered stabbing Raymond, the man who infected Dorette, and thinking how he had rid the world of one bit of scum.

He thought of how he had inadvertently got involved with Raymond's wife, unaware of whom she was. He thought about how through her, Raymond had gotten his revenge from beyond the grave.

The thought of Raymond intensified the desire to inflict physical pain and he balled his hands into a fist and punched the face before him, smashing its nose. Blood spurted and she screamed. That riled him even further. He desperately wanted to keep pounding but he had to do something about the din she was creating.

He placed one hand over her mouth in an effort to muffle her wails. With the other hand he pulled her over to the television set in the corner and turned it on, cranking the volume up hoping that the noise would further mask the sound of her terrified wails.

As he dragged her back toward the bed, a familiar voice that once whispered sweet nothings in his ear permeated the room. It had a strangely calming effect and he felt compelled to listen.

"Life doesn't end with AIDS. We can still continue to live useful, productive lives with just a few lifestyle changes."

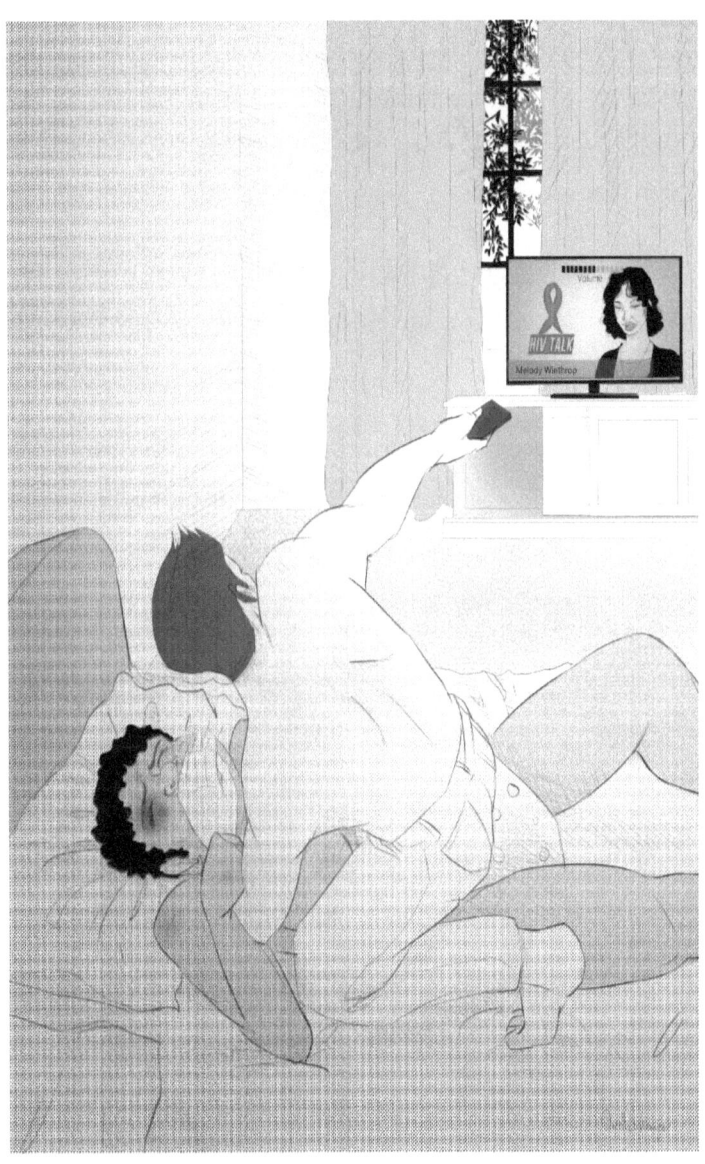

"Constance Chance, looking as composed and beautiful …"

He glanced over at the television screen. Constance Chance, looking as composed and beautiful as ever, looked back at him, her words spoken as though she were trying to reach him specifically.

Suddenly, unexplainably, he was overwhelmed by remorse. He turned to the young lady whose sobbing was beginning to recede but who was still rigid with fear.

"I am sorry. I don't know what possessed me to do that." His voice was gentle and genuinely contrite. "I want to watch this, will you join me?" he asked.

Subdued but still wary, she sat with him on the edge of the bed, in a room rancid with the odors of too many illicit encounters and too few cleanings, watching as a smart looking woman on the television tell the sad story of how she was infected.

Mark hung his head. He gently took the hand of the young girl next to him and held it.

"HIV/AIDS has no name, face or status. Unlike people, it does not discriminate. Nobody would believe that I am HIV positive but I am. Take the time to protect yourself. Life is more important than a few moments of pleasure." The woman urged.

"Let's get out of here. I'm HIV positive." Mark told the bewildered young girl beside him.

* * *

Mark, his mind a harbor of heavy thoughts, lay on his bed staring unseeingly at the ceiling. Why hadn't he killed himself? He had killed Raymond, hadn't he? He had appointed himself Raymond's judge and jury, an angel of death. Yet, when faced with similar circumstances, hadn't he done the same thing? In fact he was worse. Raymond Chance at least reserved his attention for consenting adults.

He on the other hand preyed on young girls, making them attractive offers, forcing himself on them, then not even delivering the promises he made.

He thought of what his life became since his diagnosis. He was angry and vengeful, only wanting to hurt and destroy. He embarked on a course that was destructive not only to himself, but to those who came into contact with him.

This had to end. He was going to end it all.

* * *

Marilyn smiled as she met Mark's eyes across the room. She was swollen with pride.

Just a few short months ago, she had fallen prey to the lure of some extra cash and an attractive, sweet talking man. His intention was to infect her. Fortunately, his epiphany had taken place at just the right moment and saved both their lives. Now he knew his life wasn't over with AIDS and she, that there was more to life than she had been willing to settle for.

They had become an inseparable team, working together to reach young people like herself.

As Mark shifted his gaze from Marilyn to the group of young people with whom they were having a session, he felt bittersweet redemption. He had gotten away with murder, he had infected so many, but now, he was dedicating his life to saving lives. In spite of all that went on before him, he couldn't help thinking that life was good and well worth living.

*   *   *

INTERTWINED

Dorielle Retemyer – Artist, Illustrator

Seneca College

Ontario, Canada

www.ashadraws.com

https://www.facebook.com/ashadraws